To Rosie –
for our most wonderful
walks in Central Park

To Daisy –
for our most wonderful
walks on Broadway

To Ella –
for our most wonderful
walks to Triangle Park

To Sam –
for our most wonderful walks
in Riverside Park

RHH

For Penelope
PB

A BRUBAKER, FORD & FRIENDS BOOK,
an imprint of The Templar Company Limited

First published in the UK
simultaneously in hardback and paperback
in 2012 by Templar Publishing,
The Granary, North Street, Dorking,
Surrey, RH4 1DN, UK
www.templarco.co.uk

ISBN 978-1-84877-253-3 (hardback)
ISBN 978-1-84877-933-4 (paperback)

Printed in China

SHADOW

ROBIE H. HARRIS

ILLUSTRATED BY

PATRICK BENSON

B||F||&||F

BRUBAKER, FORD & FRIENDS

AN IMPRINT OF THE TEMPLAR COMPANY LIMITED

LOOK!

LOOK AT THAT!

It's big.

It's really big.

It's TOO big.

It's BIGGER than ME.

So if I tiptoe behind it —
it won't see me.

WOW!

It's tiptoeing too.

Bet if I run away from it —

it won't get me.

OH MY GOODNESS!

I'd better hide behind this tree

so it can't find me.

I wonder if it's hiding too…

I think I'll take a little peek.

I think I'll wave at it.

LOOK!

It's waving at me.

What if I twirl around?

What if I swirl around?

WOW!

It's twirling with me.

It's swirling with me.

HEY...

let's wiggle our hips!

Stomp our feet!

Spin so fast

it makes us dizzy!

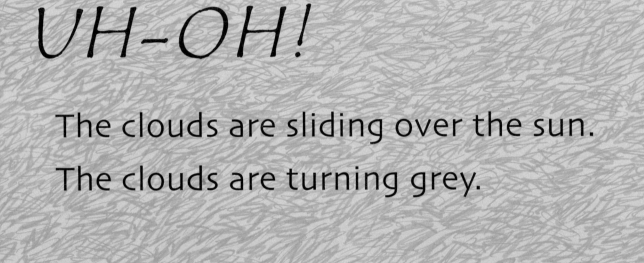

UH-OH!

The clouds are sliding over the sun.

The clouds are turning grey.

OH NO!

It's disappearing.

It's barely there at all.

NO! NO!

I don't want it to go.

OKAY!

If I make a wish —

maybe it will stay.

If I throw it a kiss —

maybe it won't go away.

OH!

I can't see it any more.

It's gone.

The day is over.

I have to go home.

I bet it's going home too.

Maybe it will come back
for supper.

Supper-time's over.

And it hasn't come back.

Bath-time's over.

And it still hasn't come back.

I didn't know I would miss it so much!

OH LOOK!

It's back.

It's here.

It came back to see me.

I just yawned.

It yawned too.

I'm tired.

It must be tired too.

And when I fall asleep —

I bet it will too.